WISE POISON

WISE POISON

DAVID RIVARD

POEMS

GRAYWOLF PRESS · SAINT PAUL

Publication of this volume is made possible in part by a grant provided by the Minnesota State Arts Board through an appropriation by the Minnesota State Legislature, and by a grant from the National Endowment for the Arts. Significant additional support has been provided by the Andrew W. Mellon Foundation, the Lila Wallace–Reader's Digest Fund, the McKnight Foundation, and other generous contributions from foundations, corporations, and individuals. Graywolf Press is a member agency of United Arts, Saint Paul. To these organizations and individuals who make our work possible, we offer heartfelt thanks.

Published by
Graywolf Press
2402 University Avenue, Suite 203
Saint Paul, Minnesota 55114

Printed in the United States of America.

ISBN 1-55597-251-9: $21.95 (cloth)
ISBN 1-55597-247-0: $12.95 (paper)

2 4 6 8 9 7 5 3 2 1
First Graywolf Printing, 1996

Library of Congress Card Catalog Number: 96-77469 (cloth)
Library of Congress Card Catalog Number: 96-75791 (paper)

Photo © 1996, Tina West, Graphistock
Cover design by Michaela Sullivan

ACKNOWLEDGMENTS

Grateful acknowledgment is made to the editors of the following publications in which the poems, sometimes in slightly different versions, first appeared. *AGNI*: "And Continuing," "The Debt"; *Antioch Review*: "Later History"; *Crazyhorse*: "Earth to Tell of the Beasts," "I Am a Pilgrim & a Stranger," "Pilgrim Lake/John Logan"; *Graham House Review*: "What Kind of Times Are They?"; *Harvard Review*: "Big Mood Swing," "Self-Portrait," "Hush & Taunt"; *Hayden's Ferry Review*: "God the Broken Lock," "It Could Be"; *Indiana Review*: "Emergency Exit," "*Fado*"; *New England Review*: "Change My Evil Ways," "Against Recovery"; *The Nebraska Review*: "The Pastoral Zone," "Version Tucson"; *The North American Review*: "Summons"; *Ploughshares*: "Little Wing," "Shy" as "The Shy," "Welcome, Fear"; *Poetry*: "*C'è Un'altra Possibilità*"; *Provincetown Arts*: "Baby Vallejo," "Mercy, Mercy"; *Red Brick Review*: "Thin Bone & Striped Feathers"; *Triquarterly*: "Curious Forces," "Jihad."

"Change My Evil Ways" appeared, in an earlier version, in *Pushcart Prize XVIII*, edited by Bill Henderson (W.W. Norton, 1993). "Earth to Tell of the Beasts," "Later History," and "Summons" appeared in the anthology *New American Poets of the 90's*, edited by Jack Myers and Roger Weingarten (David R. Godine, 1991). "And Continuing" was printed in the Poetry Society of America Newsletter as the winner of the 1990 Celia B. Wagner Award and in the anthology *What Will Suffice: The Ars Poetica in American Poetry*, edited by Christopher Buckley (Peregrine Smith, 1995).

The passage quoted in "Camus" is from the preface to *Lyrical and Critical Essays* by Albert Camus (Vintage/Random House, 1970). Reprinted with the permission of Alfred A. Knopf, Inc.

I am grateful to the National Endowment for the Arts, the Massachusetts Cultural Council, and the Somerville Arts Council for support while I was at work on this book.

My thanks to friends in Cambridge & Vermont & elsewhere for their affection & help. The title of this book owes its life to Chris McGrath.

CONTENTS

for Tony Hoagland

CAMUS

But circumstances helped me.
To correct a natural indifference,
I was placed halfway between poverty and the sun.
Poverty kept me from thinking
all was well
under the sun and in history;
the sun taught me
that history was not everything.

I

EMERGENCY EXIT

We are only being human on a Monday afternoon.

And I'm afraid, but of something that is almost nothing.

All I wanted was to be
a little headless — heedless — to be distracted today,
attentive to two people twenty feet tall
on a white screen, two blurry aficionados of the martial arts
making love on a disheveled bed, who are themselves ignorant
of the elaborate joke the man's father tells
before an offended criminal
with a razor slices his palm
and pours whiskey into the wound.

There's plenty to be afraid of, large & small.

No one here will acknowledge failure
has been driven away like a wolf
on a streetcar, temporarily,
its return about to be announced by a faint yowl
disguised as synthesizer & guitar.

But I doubt I would ever feel so
off-key with the air
that like the woman across the aisle
I would tap a chrome-blue tuning fork
against my leg, as if perched
on an icy comet,
tenaciously, a posture too tender to sing
either flamenco or Brahms.

The kids who snuck into the movie & grew bored
before the woman in a blue bra started
energetically pumping the sawed-off into her enemy's forehead,

they left by the emergency exit,
walked through the parking lot, & crossed the freeway.

One will head toward the meatpacking district, over the river.
One will make it only as far as the mountain meadow, the lupine.
One will climb the fence around a rocket launching pad.
One will sleep on grates, eloquent as an air brake.

I would like to save them all,
or at least the Buddhists seem to believe
it would be a good thing
if I wanted to. Also encouraged
is that these children should find some way to save
me.

Maybe you are the kind of person who imagines
both things might happen. If so, perhaps
you were attentive, earlier, to how the fat guy
in the front row snuffled loudly
while plonking an empty popcorn carton on his head.

A sign was what you took it as, requiring compassion.

Who are you? Where do you live?

WELCOME, FEAR

For one thing I'm glad
the goal of enlightenment means being stupid
enough to slip out the door
each morning & live. With no second-guessing,
no poses,
just this leaning & slouching
the experts term hope.
So people like me cannot be held guilty.
In our travels
we'd never laugh at the passing streets,
we're not like those grins they have
plastered to the sides of every bus.
But what do I do, what am I supposed to
do when I want someone
to hold me? How easy it is, & inevitable
and paramount & sweet, to recall
how you would dress before the mirror—
in those minutes before a blouse
started to button itself on,
when sunlight from the window might rest
briefly on your back, & I'd begin
by tipping my mouth to your skin
the way the first imagined oar dipped
into an unimaginable sea.

Now nothing seems right. Between us everything
either finished or unfinishable.
Whatever I once wrote to you fills me,
torn into many small pieces. Sometimes
it seems as if that mirror I mentioned
has been lost, perhaps stolen, but by men I'd hired

myself, mistakenly.
I am my own bad influence.
Many things have gone wrong.
And I will never be what you wished me to be.
You will always lean toward the mirror,
putting on lipstick, kissing the air,
but since the mirror has been revoked
the kiss collects in the shape of space attempting
to kiss itself. Well
the tragic can go fuck itself. Even if, once,
in the middle of the night, I woke
because a smoke detector went off, signaling
its batteries were dying. Even if it's like that. Fear,
like that: walking naked
through a cold house, moving from alarm
to alarm, unable to find the right one. Even if it's like that.

SELF-PORTRAIT

I live my life
in ways entirely forgotten
or never even known
by this hornet, this dead-since-summer yellow jacket,
its bronze husk resting
on the windowsill. A secret & clever recklessness
has always helped me. The sort that in 1953
drove a Hungarian recording engineer
to bootleg his favorite bebop & R & B.
The outlawed tunes were pressed on top of x-ray sheets.
The x rays stolen from a Budapest hospital
so a diamond-tipped stylus could glide
the bluesy decrescendos, the riffs
and splintered eighth notes, of jawbone & hip socket.
Songs from the year I was born, a cunning
that sounded something like my own
by the time I turned twenty, my birthday
the spring night
I shoved a friend's VW van down an embankment
and into the estuary. It was our plan
to cop her insurance, & finance a trip to Mexico.
After the splash, a rustling
in bayberry and cottonwood, lapping waves,
mosquito silence.
When she heard the police sent down divers,
searching for bodies, she cried.
If, after placing my hand on her cheek
and touching those tears,
I'd raised my fingers to my lips,
their saltiness might have humbled me.
I didn't. I kept my own counsel,
always acting
generous & satisfied, an impersonator
of the helpful, my plots & schemes

disguised. The other hornet knows how,
the slyer one, the one who spotted
a hole in the screen, & dared to squeeze through.
He flew off to join the next dance
around a branch of overripe pears, he was
a daydreamer, & easily distracted—by a day-old smear of ketchup,
by sweat-dampened hair—dreaming
of sailing downstream
on a chip of cedar bark,
wings folded back, lost, but canny enough
not to give the feeling a name.

I AM A PILGRIM & A STRANGER

In the one small clearing
between the tag end of
an endorphin spike & a ragged
pulse-tone emitted
by his heart monitor,
uncomprehending, hopeless, rueful,
paid of recrimination, my father
wants, again, to roll up
the pastel pajama leg
and show me the ulceration
that pits his thigh.
I have no more arguments,
on the fifth of twenty-six
floors for compliance & denial
at Brigham & Women's Hospital.
I can't even hold his hand.
Nothing to be afraid of?
An amber circle rims
and measures the ulcer.
Bruise purple at the edge,
hub & core gray
as axle grease, the skin
crusts with scabs.
Look long, alone,
and it's like staring hard
into the sun; turn away,
the afterimage burns
on your retina, a negative,
another more restless
and weary eye
blankly glaring back.
Clench shut your lids,
it tracks inside your head.
Not God's eye, since he's

withdrawn from the universe
and spot-welded the seams,
leaving all his laws
inside to gear the engine.
Not pain's, or pride's,
but the eye of a pilgrim
and wanderer, for whom
earth is only a windstruck
and lonely ridge overlooking
cities sprawled below
on a plain the color of straw.
What have I seen, what have I seen
I have not let go of & only loved?

ANY WHERE OUT OF THE WORLD

And then there are places
no one ever expects to arrive.
From San Francisco once
a man led hundreds of followers
to Guyana, on chartered cargo ships,
though later
he would instruct them to swallow sugar water
laced with strychnine. It was a clearing
of simply carpentered houses, of covetous mongrels,
nicknames, clean laundry,
and off-key singing. Kool-Aid,
a communal settlement in the jungle, a town
that after an accretion of reenactments
on television & in the pitying words
of various commentators
became a mind
collapsing in on itself, finally dense enough.
And isn't each of us rich enough
with losses, with disasters?
                              When I first heard the name
Jonestown, the news was handed me,
with Mexican shock
and skepticism, by a janitor
sweeping the airport lounge
in Mérída. Should I say
I felt remorse, or disgust, rancor,
or just a little shaky? November in the Yucatán,
short of cash, I had slept the night
in a stony field outside the terminal,
barely nodding off, sweating ferociously in a down mummy bag
as inappropriate for the lowland heat
as the shirt I'd been wearing,

a heavy, ornately woven cloth
dyed violet-purple by Mayan mestizos.
It had cost me
a week of haggling in an Atitlán *mercado*.
That morning, in the men's room,
after stripping off the shirt,
I found my chest & arms tinted
a translucently purplish red
paper towels and liquid soap couldn't scrub off—
so that the words the janitor spoke
seemed then to have made my body
glow, like a particle shot
scraping through dense air, one of the brief
phosphor-red sparks thrown off
by an emery wheel
while someone sharpens a blade.

WHAT KIND OF TIMES?

What kind of times? When we still seem to want
      what we've already gotten,
influence & coin, acumen & verve, got, & given

again whatever's due us after getting, the esteem,
      the song, the necessary
snakeskin, the necessary drug, say six breeds

of dog that insinuate power, or the tan of her
      shoulders, a meticulous tan, & silk
black & loose as it falls from her shoulders.

Whatever it is, without completion or calm.
      What can never be enough.
Whether you stand on the curb at First & 6th,

snapping an imaginary whip, or the gift possessed
      by your hands begins
to recede, the stalk of hyacinth, freshly cut,

its scent, unlikely to overwhelm for longer
      than a beat. If you breathe here
now. In the praxis of attainables. American.

CURIOUS FORCES

The party spills outside, & for a short time, overhead,
the stars look trapped, like travelers attacked
by bandits, but dead-drunk, so loaded
they hardly act surprised. The air cool,
though I don't want a coat. And none would fit anyway,
nothing in the closet looks familiar, everything—
even my leather jackets—seems shrunk.
As if the rains got endless. As if my greatcoat,
the camel hair my brother loaned, smartened-up
and stalked back to him. But you were the one
who ripped the raglan sleeves,
and snapped off all the buttons.
Sometimes for one last time I am
the small space between your tongue & lips,
a December morning, tears, our teeth chattering.
Even then, I don't want a coat, & don't now.
And isn't this the way it always starts—without need,
first going out coatless, then
joking, the way I do, offering for five bucks
to buy a thirty-year-old blazer,
the olive-gold & green-that-is-mostly-
a-bewitching-black polyester worn by a woman
who resembles you
only if she whispers. The silk lining is ripped,
the lapels stained by wine in one or two places.
When will my life begin again?
Sometimes your smile drifts through my veins,
a raft I float to safety on. I stand outside on a wooden deck,
offering to buy a jacket.
Tenderness is amazed.
The deck descends toward the river.
And you are two thousand miles away,
while my sad cough, my indigenous sadness, loiters,

stuck, on some nearby stairs.
In Tucson, once, there was a man who
thinking you turned tricks
came over to your table & left his business card,
all because of a leopard-skin skirt & makeup.
How blank his breath as you threw back the card,
the lettering raised & black.
Sometimes I have wished to be that card. Tonight
I ask too many questions of the woman
I stand with, her blond, centripetal hair enlivening
the curious forces of the party, & of course
I make another offer on her jacket,
as if donning it might make me clear enough
to understand if our marriage had ended,
if I were really leaving you
and the love of the last twelve years.
Sometimes I have wished to be
ink, black on white, & flung.

THE DEBT

Dignity exists I'm sure,
and because this is Rhodes it must be
kissed by the same pentecostal wind
swaying the palms, the histamine yellow light warming
stones, even if
behind the lobby bar
a Belgian named René stands,
clowning, pouring, wiping, talking,
talking his bartender chat. It is only later, later
in the consuming lime & gin of the later,
when he mentions the debt,
incurred by gambling, perhaps — keeping it vague — sneaking in
some explanation at any rate for how he finds himself
unable to return to his previous life.
His cot is visible through the open pantry door,
and on a shelf next to it, by the hot plate,
a bottle of Luminol for migraines.
But the blackness of his earring, a single pearl,
severs itself from light,
as if to corroborate the fact that
after his debts were paid off
by the owner of this C-class pensione,
and his passport taken as collateral,
he went to work here
as bartender, porter, night clerk,
and maid, a kind of
indentured servant,
with a five-year contract. The first provision of which asserts
somebody might manage to live
purposefully by hauling the aluminum-white smoke
of Gauloises into his lungs,
his brain packed in pharmaceuticals
like a new camera crammed snug into a Styrofoam carton
and shipped off to an unknown address,

the carton handled as carefully
as a common box turtle picked up
by a slightly malicious, mildly curious
child, who, having spotted it navigating a tidal marsh—
small flippers, leathery slo-mo paddles, wriggling
over the shallows & through
the kelp—grabs the turtle
and ties it atop scrap from a wooden lobster trap,
launching the raft
out into the pond, where the current takes it
down the cut & quickly, dutifully,
abandons it to the waves.

SUMMONS

Suppose I can convince myself this
world is my home only by claiming it
could never be & then assuming we all
share that feeling, a bond that anchors us
each to the planet, even those hired
to populate this photo, spread across
pages twenty-four & twenty-five, a beach
party, & the magazine scented because
what else should summon us to delusion
but perfume, drifting up from the tanned
and fiercely healthy faces, a massaged glow,
in precise attunement to the means
implied by the Queen Anne porch & gables,
women in summer evening dresses, barefoot,
heels tossed in clumps of eel grass, lightly
wavering stalks, & two men in tuxes
about to heap driftwood atop a bonfire
while a third lugs the straw hamper of food
and wines, the models' laughter unheard
but booming out over dunes & waves,
joyful efflorescent laughing, easy to envy,
and hidden inside their shouts another shot
of them, later, clothes stripped off, drunken,
running down the beach into a warm
plankton-lit surf, since these are the seas
out of which we once evolved crawling
and skittering over one another's backs.

AGAINST GRAVITY

Blue sky, ungated clouds, & on a sand-pitted
highway sign the number 10 stands out —
a minor footnote in a monograph on drugs,

a reference instructing the reader to study
my nap on the floor of a Ford Econoline
summer after high school. As if rest, & only rest,

were what we found ourselves made of, sometimes.
Though rest is only one trait, actually, when
you've been hitching between Tucson & El Paso

and gotten picked up by a van. The equally ingenious
others look like tie-dye & restlessness, like
rest stops & silvered heather, maybe jimson,

and a little lantana raising its nippled red speckles
into the scent of sagebrush rained on & drying.
They got me high, three men & a woman costumed

estimably in the style of out-of-work jesters,
jovial people of 1971, wearing the standard issue —
fusty cloches, velveteen pants, embroidered emblems,

with shiny balls like cat bells dangling
off one or two ears. For one a self-etched tattoo,
its motto the equation ACID=BLISS framed

by a multiplying fungus or exploding chloroplast.
For another, a Fu Manchu & fedora. A synaptic Apache
snake cinching the woman's frayed macramé belt.

Mirror sunglasses for all. And small mirrors,
like tiny ponds, frozen pools, had been sewn
onto the woman's India print blouse by some

Kashmiri laborer, who, if he could have looked into
them, might have seen me dozing off, stoned
on pan hash, bits of myself reflecting back,

scattered, a tired grin from the woman's
right sleeve, the puffed wrist, pale ear at the tip
of a breast, nose on her stomach. And haven't I

always loved being broken up & abrogated by sleep?
But when I woke we had pulled off the road
into a ranch. From the tape deck "Brain Salad Surgery"

blared, a form of premature senility disguised
as endless synthesizer riffs. For a second, in the nazz
and compression of noise, still stoned, I thought

they intended to kill me. An intuition
so melodramatic & dumb the sight of two of the men
kissing in the front seat had to wipe it away.

I had never seen two men kiss, & the surprise,
which in another setting might have shocked,
even disgusted, my sheltered murmurous little self,

somehow reassured me. The kiss implying
not so much gentility as distraction.
Then, out of the eddies of shade, the woman

ran, having tossed off her incongruous imitation
alligator heels, naked now except for
purple tights, she ran & turned cartwheels

three times across the yard. Gravity.
Gravity. They had wanted to visit a friend
who, they claimed, was connected to anti-

gravity research being conducted there.
Merely a windbreak occupied by
an adobe shed and barn, it seemed abandoned,

as if during the night the hard rains,
the lightning, had chased away the enemy
of gravity, & now we were to take his place.

HUSH & TAUNT

There,
the story starts & ends, *he & the woman*
lived awhile. Almost another life. His
betrayals, & laughter. Mint, & the salt fog.
His heart, unsure.
Sometimes, long after the river darkened
at evening, rippling where the weir lights struck,
he liked to stand on the cottage porch,
studying the surface, watching
the tide as it covered the pilings,
waiting. From the living room,
a voice, an untamed calm, Bob Marley's
hush & taunt headlong over the guitars.

Nights
waitressing the cocktail lounge
she drove home around three.
Her hair pulled back, braided into the long auburn rope
occasionally tugged on by drunks.
Across the river, strobe lights blinked
on the power-plant stacks, & a breeze nagged furnace smoke
over an orchard, while, below,
the invisible apple & pear boughs, in blossom,
glistened.
               Or might have,
if all the discredited probabilities, the leaps
of the romantic, had still
been in effect.
               But, regardless,
he liked to draw the bath, & watch her.
What did he want,
and then again what did he want
to tell her?
Was it the little dance of desire water did

trickling jaw to collarbone? The leniency,
the taste of skin
along the neck? Or the gesture
she made rising from the tub,
like a candle guttering & flaring back
twice as bright? There was
no telling.
        Lucky for her she left later,
moved to El Paso.
           And of the loud wind
outside their window, make what you wish — maybe
the sound of turbines, on the far shore,
venting steam — but I heard it as the future,
inured, speeding, certain
it will always outlast the past, & wanting
only . . .

SHY

We even breathed shyly, envying everybody
their courage & finesse. Everybody's boldness
a little inebriating. But even drunk
we had no nerve, we were
patient, much too patient, like
old men, & overrehearsed, frowners, fishermen
who for hours practiced
fly casting in the park,
each cast erasing the future
of streams
and flame-spotted trout.
We could have asked for risks
but blushed at our clumsiness, our imperfections
like lamps of oil
lit just beneath the skin.
Shamefaced. Rosy. Reddened.
Look, look.
There must have been
many hours like coal mines,
very dark & confusing, dripping & quiet & cold,
which required that light.
We outfitted ourselves, with modesty & doubt.
Delighted to be
mispronouncing words, mangling our speech.
Whole days lived as if caught
dreaming beneath an elm
in light rain
where the sidewalk remains dry,
reliving some disgrace or humiliation
simple as absentmindedness.
Because what would shyness have been
without shyness? Without it
there might have been calm.
The green of the elm no longer

ruffling leaves. The street
quiet, the motorbikes & cars banished
with the sudden grace of dolphins,
and the rain ended, a lull,
in which a mouse might pause,
about to devour
a live cat, playing with it for
just a while longer.

DOCUMENT PROCESSING

Not the Chilean debt restructuring, not
even the pro bono for San Quentin prisoners, & certainly
none of the venture sheets, the start-ups in gene splicing.
None of it loved us. Twenty-four floors below,
the Embarcadero, impudent,
the neon pagodas & coffee-roasting plants, melancholy.
The fog erasing bridges & bay.
But it never blanked the legal docs I proofed,
so, lights off,
three or four of us, the night shift, slouched in attorneys' chairs,
our midnight lunch break
in the law firm's unadorned, Politburo-gray
glass & Formica conference room. Where, occasionally,
one of the document processors, a woman,
would entertain. She said,
at home, coming from some of the other
apartments, there were little moans, she heard them
through her kitchen window. And we all loved her voice,
its connivance & submersion, a dark glint
because the men & women she imagined
making love never were the real tenants
but people she pulled together
from other places & times —
whoever had loved enough, whoever had not.
The clerk from a Palo Alto bookstore,
the slur of her blond long hair across the nipples of a man
she'd seen throw a painting into a dumpster.
The ones in 3H, brothers who painted barracks
on a military post, they masturbated for their wives.
The document processor told us. She said little moans,
persuasive slatherings, light slaps
like spanking, or like slaps, altercations, short cries,
and louder moans, snaps undone, & giggled
clichés, & every so often

the shiver of smudged instruction, of fabric, the breath
of a wet command, annoyance, zippers,
endearment, coaxing, ripping, wheedling.

That noisy? Of course not, no, but augmented,
prolonged in the privacy of my blood, my brain.
And now you think I'm telling some secret about myself.
I did after all move from body to body, borrowing.
Why be stuck staying one person—
a mouthful of hopes, a handful of denials?

She brought together whoever she felt
most needful & polished, or inept & thrilled.
The work product rippled across our desks,
currency agreements, development bankruptcies.
And we drifted along,
we pictured her at a stove frying onions
and leaning nearer the window, listening to two women
she'd watched at a rugby game,
the Marina green. The asbestos litigation,
the conveyance of profit margins, the deeding
of cattle empires, of windmill projects.
The singer—at the BART station he was loud, a heckler,
at home polite, because the waitress, a Moroccan, wanted him
submissive. It was always after arriving
from work, she said, or as she got ready to go.
But some of you might care more
that on those nights she had no stories we improvised
through the nearly deserted offices & corridors
a course for mini-golf,
knocking the ball around ficus trees & computer stations,
playing carpet holes & cigarette burns as water hazards,
file folders as sand traps. The building swayed
in wind & light earthquakes. A temblor of 5.3, & imperceptibly

the dimpled ball rolled. 6.4, & my curiosity
surprised, revolving. 3.7, I lost interest
in my own inhibitions. On clear nights
Sausalito smeared the hilly black horizon
with its imitation of sparks, a mercenary army's encampment,
fires of the victors & vanquished.
Whoever wished could try to pick out the lights
of the split-level where a young broker drowned a woman
he'd hired to fuck bound & gagged in a bathtub,
his wife & children off visiting.
Now you think I'm telling you innocence flares
only as its potential for destruction & self-indictment,
as if there were too many games.
But there aren't enough.
Their purpose is always to reflect. To mirror the darker leathers,
the worn & unworn, the mouth marks that stain
the skin for a day or two, to mimic the speechless
plural of glances, swellings, a drunken
gentle attendance, the ungentle. You think I'm telling you
something naive, or wrong, but I don't exist
except as an absolute distrust of words,
a dark trinket you can wear, & finger,
while you decide what you most want, the care, or the taunts,
whichever you think
you're getting, the strappado or the luxuries, whatever
is unexpected, the windows
raised & wanton & wanting.
You know the ones.

THE PASTORAL ZONE

As if all day a child had penciled & erased
on blond vellum, scrub pine on the bluff

above Drake's Beach comes & goes in the fog.
My shirt loose in the breeze, a plum-colored skirt

that swirls around your legs: the shadows on shag grass
look like us, but aren't. The way they flicker

they're more like the marsh wrens crowding the rail
of this wooden fence. The way our hands touch,

the best loneliness is ours, as well as the worst.
Which is it that makes you smile & forget?

The day is like wet burning wood. Gray & blue
west across the ordinary meadowlife of August,

all the way back down the footpath: Guernseys,
hay bales, vineyard, weathered apple orchard,

weathered tractor & baler come & go
in the fog. Each time we look at the ocean,

and the wind drops, all that's left is the song
of the marsh wrens, musical sewing machines:

how, gradually, what cannot be mended
is mended. That won't stop us feeling alone

when we shut our eyes. Even here where
the weather & salt air smear us together,

together, two shadows, two talented passions.
And though for a second we can't tell which is

which, one is more like the wind licking foxtail,
and the other like a stalk, bending, bending.

VERSION TUCSON

Above a cloud of stick-spears a stabbed ibis darts,
careening on stubby, foil-bright wings.

Or else a woman bows to horned bison, just as they leap a cliff.

And you would think that what flickers in these paintings
is thanks, gouged into the limestone of the cave:
praise for meat, for tinder & companions
and rivers, praise for light
and the privilege of striding its meadows.
That's one interpretation.
                              But it's the other version, our beginnings
rendered as defiance, or pride, that excuses
the place inside me where a wall stands,
yellowish stucco, flaking, with bougainvillea,
three straggly runners
arcing a pair of blue-framed windows,
and a helicopter, the police, hovering above, poking
a searchlight around.
I stood next door.
In a while, the blades droned off, fading.
Under the branches of tamarack & mock orange then
quiet, like a windless pond—
into which was tossed a voice,
swearing, quietly, cursing who knows what,
my neighbor, a roofer whose wife had two days earlier
taken the kids & driven to Seattle,
scared by his drunks & abuse.
                              I remember standing there
that night—I was outside because of something,
what? nothing terrible, an imaginary illness
with an imaginary cure, a mood—I was

calm, wary, just listening to this man, this bitterness
walking the world as a carpenter — that was his job,
not roofing — a carpenter's mouth & tongue,
his fingernails and eyes, like splinters & chips of spite
all nailed together. But I wasn't alone,
there were other witnesses, the cholla & saguaro,
the swing set, water sprinklers, crushed beetles
and tattered lawn chairs. All of them
silent too. Except now
they could admit what I won't, they could rob me
of my alibi
and accuse me of smiling, at one point,
and thinking myself lucky.

IT COULD BE

the same stale wind
I felt on Muscungus Bay,

the August breeze ruffling
a stuffed toy, the bobbing grubby Minnie Mouse
some lobstermen left behind, strung
by her neck
from a rust-abraded navigational buoy.
Her forehead, belly & shriveled arms
tattooed by crudely drawn swastikas.
With her stitching torn too,
so whenever exhaust blew from the idling
outboard into our eyes
the cotton batting looked as if it were foaming out.

That air.

Perhaps
only because I have forgotten
the struggle between anguish
and anguish, that air
is what jet-streams toward me today.
A wind that bitters any scorn of fear, it would wipe out
all our ways of warding off the danger.
Gust whose threat would smash our names
to syllables, the syllables
into letters, & letters
into kindling, splintered spruce.

Last night, when a man jogged by
in the falling snow
wearing spandex dyed the tint of ripened lemons,
with matching headband,
I saw him as a snowflake

might—his shape
that of an animal whittled
sloppily from a chunk of pine,
the whiter, sweetish pulp of the tree
where love feels it cuts deepest.
Painted a baffled yellow
with one or two black stripes, his legs were wobbly,
the hooves rushing over ground covered
by snow, slipping, the earth
a ball of muddy soil, hand-packed, frozen,
hanging in blackness, held by a flimsy red thread,
the kind used to tear open
a Band-Aid wrapper.

BABY VALLEJO

Take the night Myron Stout shut his sure blind eyes,
his pale head tilted back awhile, smiling
and swaying to an Eric Dolphy solo, or that morning
a sea otter, having fed, preened in the cove
below Tomales Bay, wolf gray & magpie black—
both times
it was easy to feel how
each left his mark on me.
Out of my happiness they carved an intensity.
Though the same might be said of my hatred.
Take the moment my grip loosened
so I couldn't stop my cousin
punching out his wife. His mark shaped
like a stony, contemptible hand,
but even its lines
flawlessly chiseled, cunning, still coaxing me,
even now, to go inside to look it over.
No matter who made them
I love each of these marks, whoever it was
whispering or shouting near me.
Nostalgia has nothing to do with it,
and neither loneliness nor grief.
Again & again I go
into myself to study them, bypassing only
that mark fashioned in June of 1976,
set there by a worried face, a phlegmy voice
asking why a bus should swerve into a crowded plaza,
a school bus, blue, gutted of seats,
soldier at the wheel. Why the washed-out
white star stenciled
on its hood? Inside, men hang by their wrists,
naked, beside two dead calves,
two flayed & stiffened carcasses
swinging on meat hooks

as the bus pulls over.
                    It was simply a dream,
and the man recounting it, a tile mason, Pakistani, wanted
only the least implausible interpretation.
But I never answered,
out of ignorance or indifference, some job-site superstition.
I stood with him, silent, at that development
where I slapped up drywall.
Hands grizzled by dried grouting pastes,
he spoke the concise, elaborated English
a former lecturer in linguistics might—
since, in fact, that is what he had once been,
that & a cipher for the wrong politics—his words filtered
through a crushed windpipe, a nose smashed
during several precisely engineered & official beatings.
Suffice it to say
the mark carved inside me by that voice
is probably exquisite, intricate,
as grave & sinuous as the graying hairs
of the beard that covered his scars.
But I don't go in to look it over.
Because he knows why
in my poems a querulous gray rain sometimes sweeps down,
and, knowing, refuses
to believe, as I do, that the roofs of our houses,
of the huts & pavilions & civic centers,
will withstand the rain's buffeting,
why, in other words,
sadly, happily, luxuriously, it is often
Rivard against Rivard.

MERCY, MERCY

No denying all the tenements & precincts
waking to betrayal, crippled hope,
though this won't be one,
a morning when I'm nine
and leaving for school. Early May,
a heavy mist, the shrubs glazed with it
like runny shellac, and
the plaster statue of Saint Francis, dripping.
I want what a drop wants
as it shivers from his chin.
A wish that, later, seems childish, wussy.
But why can't I become the cat too? Her stupid pleasure,
her two yellow teeth jutting
because grackles crowd the power lines,
the raucous fist-thick cable sagging, incarnate,
obedient as any thing alive
to gravity.
Always & anywhere I believe a wish
is as obedient as every living thing.
So not just the cat, but the lilacs too,
soggy, trembling lightly in the breeze,
like grazing beasts, bowed to mulch,
I could be their trembling.
Or, trying harder, squeeze
into the wiry, stoop-shouldered body
of my neighbor, on his way
to punch in at the grain mill.
He'll listen to the rats
scatter when he powers up
the conveyor. The rats
quick to hide, only to return at dusk,
hunched under the long canvas belt,
come again for the mercy of a world
they can't help but trust
will always feed them.

CHANGE MY EVIL WAYS

Some days it is my one wish to live
alone, nameless, unfathomable,
a drifter or unemployed alien.
But that day the movie was over.
I found myself walking
in Cambridge, & on the Common
there were some conga players, as well as the guys
with xylophones, with fingerpianos & tambourines.
Have you ever seen minnows flopping
from shallow to shallow, doing somersaults?
The drummers' hands were pale fish,
like guppies thrashing light in a clear plastic bag,
as blurred as children careening around
lawn sprinklers in the careening mercuric blue dusk of August.
Dulse wavering! Hair shook out while somebody dances.
Some days it isn't a life alone I need
but one that supplies the luxury
of forgiveness. It was a day like that,
luckily. Past the tobacconist,
a kid sang his song about changing
my evil ways, & strummed
a three-chord blues, plugged into a boom box
that lay at his side like a wolfhound.
And I put my ear close to his snout,
and—a little
cautious at first—I began to listen.

LITTLE WING

Of all the questions
I have been lucky enough to ask
only one wants to know whose
feelings are most like my own—
just as easily
a way of asking
whose are not.
                    Like those soft
scented brushes flourished hastily
over the back of your neck after a haircut,
some feelings, some of
mine, are too obvious
to notice, or distracting, disturbingly
vague in their swath of powder & sable.
This one is like loneliness.
It could be everyone feels it
walking the ruins
at Land's End, the Sutro baths where
sixty years ago, winter & summer,
the nine mosaic-tiled saltwater pools filled
with swimmers
stroking along, bobbing, stroking.
Until the night the palladium dome,
an intricate Victorian lattice
of timber & glass, burned,
and was razed. The cement sluices,
the ducts for the ocean water
crumbling now, sewn with pondweed & widgeon grass.

A pleasing loneliness, don't doubt it,
to walk where so many swam.
Back & forth, under the sun.
All on my own I drift, & drift off.

The grandson
of a man & a woman who sweltered

in the pitch-humid sheds of the Connecticut Valley
rolling tobacco into cheap cigars,
I am never surprised to hear
in the astral & swampy songs of a cardinal
an undertone of cheerfully French gloom.
So suppose the melancholy Quebecois ballads they sang
fluttered past the heavy, resinous leaves
and, absorbed by each other's genes,
encased & coded,
passed down to me.
                    Then
my loneliness might need to be
protected,
by everyone else's.

BIG MOOD SWING

For the last few weeks I haven't refused any, not
a single feeling, not one, I haven't
failed to bow toward each for hours,
to speak enormously with each for at least the minimum
minutes. And didn't my feelings do the same,
in return? Wasn't it
a tender & brotherly translation?
I wore the sweater my father gave me, weeping.
I stood near the cargo hangars, daydreaming
a woman, her skin, her pale arms
bare. Her cool, surprising skin
at the beginning
of spring, its zealous style.
So many feelings, & as usual sometimes
too many, & many confusions. I danced,
as ecstatic & hopeful as
a cartoon, or afraid, some nights
worried I might fail.
But the alarm always rang,
so I woke in time to hate a plastic bag
caught in the crown of a poplar—
this bag that refused to be torn apart
by wind—it was my anger the bag fought,
my resentment against the black & red
Stop & Shop lettering, the weekly meat & poultry special,
the sober photos of unsuspecting children
who'd been lost or stolen.
I couldn't exempt myself
or skip out & act derelict,
but because it smelled like April, April in Chile,
there were pears to taste again. In the streets,
I saw sunlight on the smoked glass of limousines,
the rivalry
of a lesser sun with greater, & there were sudden

showers, soundless knives, even a fireman
wearing fur, his singing,
or was that singeing?
And after all that,
I still can't tell you
who I am, though I can imagine his greeting,
and how it sounds
much as these words would
if they were whispered by two people
exchanging rings, before they turned to the crowd
and, over the mortgaged, green & muddy fields,
waved their hands.

for Dean Young

III

GOD THE BROKEN LOCK

I've died enough by now I trust
just what's imperfect or ruined. I mean God,
God who is in the stop sign
asking to be shotgunned, the ocean that evaporates even
as we float. God the bent nail & broken lock,
and God the hangnail. The hangnail.
And a million others might be like me, our hopes
a kind of illegal entry, a belief in smashed windows,
every breakage
like breaking & entering into a concert hall,
the place my friend & I crawled into an air shaft, & later
fell asleep. After breakage
there is always sleep.
We woke to gospel hymns from the dressing room
below, songs commending
embrace to the fists, & return to the prodigal.
And hasn't my luck always been a shadow, stepping out, stretching?
I mean I trust what breaks.
A broken bone elicits condolence,
and the phone call sounds French if the transmission fritzes,
and our brains—our blessed, desirable brains—are composed
of infinitesimal magnets, millions of them
a billionth-of-a-milligram in weight, so
they make us knock our heads against hard walls.
When we pushed through the air vent,
the men singing seemed only a little surprised,
just slightly freaked,
three of them in black tuxes, & the fourth in red satin,
crimson, lit up like a furnace trimmed with paisley swirls,
the furnace of a planet, or of a fantastic ocean liner
crisscrossing a planet we've not discovered yet,
a fire you might love to be thrown into.
That night they would perform the songs half

the country kept on its lips half of every day.
Songs mostly praising or lamenting or accusing some loved one
of some beautiful, horrendous betrayal or affection.
But dressing, between primping & joking about
their thinning afros, they sang of Jesus. Jesus,
who said, "Split a stick, & you shall find me inside."
It was the winter we put on asbestos gloves, & flameproof
stuck our hands in the fireplace, adjusting logs.
Jesus, we told them, left no proof of having sung a single note.
And that, said the lead singer, is why we all are sinners.
What he meant was
we are all like the saints on my neighbors' lawns —
whose plaster shoulders & noses,
chipped cloaks & tiaras, have to be bundled
in plastic sheets, each winter, blanketed
from the wind & the cold. That was what he meant,
though I couldn't know it then.

for Rick Jackson

EARTH TO TELL OF THE BEASTS

Because it's summer a trellis of Gulf air curves over the day,
buckling, resiny.
    6:30 one morning,
you killed yourself.
     And in one of the minutes since then
I'm drawn to the porch by a ripsaw's
E-flat run through plywood, a crude lullaby
about shelter & endurance. Between cuts, from the shade
of a hawthorn, a jay whistles
the sassy hymns & palpitations
fate will never be able to outlaw.
      So, ears filled by all
this singing, fate cowers, & trembles,
and agrees to the erasure of every word placing your Toyota
on Maui, parked off a cliff road. Words like *the syringe*,
your deft fingers tying
off, & shooting, while flames eat the wick of rags
you stuffed in the gas tank. A junkie,
but not only that. As for mercy, when the gas ignites
no words will be allowed to flare outward with the explosion,
each syllable elided that would scorch
clumps of fuchsia, fleshy leaves of wild ginger.
      It's a good bet.
It's easy. A sure thing. That the warmth & abiding
plenitude of this morning would permit me
to call your pain a fugue, an intricately feathered
spiral, because it sounds lovely. And lovely implies consolation
and accuracy. But all the while, buried inside, hurt
is still hurt, shame still shame.
     And though you turned, once,
at the edge of a pool in Tucson, green eyes intensified
by the water, snub nose pierced by a tiny silver stud, gossiping,

you would never have claimed
your laughter was a music, as I could now,
the run of notes
a stampede, & after the stampede just tracks in the earth
to tell of the beasts & their escape.

AGAINST RECOVERY

It's true, my expectations did
often get out of control, & do, & in fact
I once assumed Los Angeles meant
not just the piers
and missional roofs, & not only the afterlife of auto parts,
but the one persuasive capital of unchallenged pleasure.
And probably I did think angels on the beach
with tequila in their tits. So what?
I *was* persuaded. But living dissolves
into events
the way the city dissolved into
things like the Christmas tree factory,
the ornaments warehouse & polyvinyl-tree farm
where we had to deliver
our car, that Buick from the suburbs
of Boston, a Drive-A-Way station wagon.
For now,
let me be none of those
or any of the other moments of my biography — none
except the prolonged surprise of waking with you,
in a Venice Beach living room empty
of all furniture save a pool table.
Why not allow the ocean waves to take everything
but you & me, & possibly the pool table,
everyone, the whole eavesdropping city & county,
even the owner
of that split-level living room, whose car
we've driven three thousand miles.
Let the cold Pacific breakers rush
over the factory he runs, & inside it
the Mexicans, the Salvadorans,
who turned toward us
worrying Immigration
when we entered. And if the desert palms

go, then so can the discounts,
the mescaline beach at dawn.
Actually, once the lifeguard towers are all gone
the water might as well rise up & take me,
starting with the mark on my forehead,
pressed in sleep against your shoulder.
Let it drown me & drag my body past the Channel Islands.
I'll come back as black cotton dotted with tiny florets,
your dress, as a tea rose
that rises along your thighs, or else
as the photo you keep in a pocket, you & your sister
walking the harbor, late in the fall.
I'll return, a strand of your hair,
a stray plume, unwoven, brash, that wishes only to lick
your lips, but gets caught there
at the corner of your mouth. Your mouth
was always naked.

C'È UN'ALTRA POSSIBILITÀ

I refuse to accept
the soul at death
shoots outward consumed
in wind & light.
More likely it arcs
back into the past,
eager to touch
every face & word,
poisons as well
as blessings. And whatever
once seemed puzzling,
a mystery, without reason,
will be clear. A long
calming look will
explain the man
at the rally in Florence,
under the red canvas
banner of the PCI.
Across it, yellow, the phrase,
c'è un'altra possibilità,
fluttering, while he
spoke to us, mumbled,
something about meeting
Dante at evening—a drunk,
or the creature who "bit
himself like one whom
fury devastates within."
His fingers, spavined,
scabbed, clenching
and unclenching when
he went off to watch
the intersection of a rower's
scull with clouds suffused
by violet & reflected at

sunset in the muddy river.
One look, to understand
his fears, each of
his confusions. And one
for the quickest & most
coaxing of your smiles,
at noon, in the square
outside Santa Croce,
where we ate.
A mother tossed
scoops of bread crumbs
on the head & shoulders
of her little boy,
and the pigeons roosting
atop all the cornices
swooped to flock
and swirl around him.
His laughter & shrieking,
it will be understood too.
And then?
Then the soul will see,
finally, how useless
wisdom is, & save itself
by being reborn.

THIN BONE & STRIPED FEATHERS

Even if it were rock
we were made of,
stone mind, stone lips,
I would still
stand here tonight
glad to go on living,
listening to a woman
say that as a child
her parents packed her
off to convent school.
Stone lips would ask
about the catechism teacher,
who chatted to herself
in Slovene. Stone mind
could picture her walking
her class to the Chrysler
Building, & the nun
pointing out a floor above
the lobby a ledge smudged
with coal smoke. The ledge
where a sparrow perched.

If that bird were to jab
its beak against the wall,
until the granite
crumbled, grain by grain,
it would take him
forever, & that, the nun
says, is how long
eternity lasts.

Maybe I would have looked
up at her then—her face
placid, dreamy, squeezed

into an oval by the starched
habit — & begun lecturing
her. My lecture?
I might have made use
of things nearly immune
to attack — like lanterns
and a certain cheap
shampoo, some books,
The Alexandria Quartet,
some uprisings, or
a little waste metal
from a drill press,
and anyone's arms
if he surf casts for blues.
But no lecture was delivered.
I was not that girl.
And this woman had her
eyes, trustful, fervent,
such a short time.
Now she seems like
the rest of us, a little
dazed, fragile, but audacious
as a wing, hollow
thin bone & striped feathers.

PILGRIM LAKE / JOHN LOGAN

Now you are just a wavering figure projected at no one's wall.

Can you recall you sang? Even shrunk
within the gabardine of an exasperated scholar.
The song wore the face of a man caught hovering
between dismay & wry amusement,
behind taped bifocals, between sorrowing amusement & merciless
shame, someone
trying to relate to you everything
he knew about coming to be healed.

And even if one day each of us will be nailed to earth,
I can't say the nails will prevent us from being restored.

Now that you have a wider perspective,
does this fen, flooded sedges with spear-long cattails,
still seem to stand for desire & guilt?
Do the dogs, barking, closing, in a nearby clump of birch,
still warn against rest?

I stood once under the Cineplex marquee at Sutter & Van Ness,
waiting for you to limp up
smiling the lopped, all-purpose grin of a stroke victim.
Boulevard & stereo shops & wholesalers of rattan & radials
and all the shoppers levitating
as fog blew in
thicker & thicker in late afternoon.

I don't know if fog corrodes the nails ultimately,
all of us left floating but dispossessed of all our fears.

But I knew you, & the mist, descendant
now over this duck-flecked pond,
soon to become a temporary, portable screen.

On it will be a flickering figure,
a bit shy perhaps
but clearly amazed.

JIHAD

I love the drops of rain that stammer down the fire escape,
the second cousins of history, as slyly incestuous as all second cousins.
Joe Reth lives below, a commercial sign painter,
wife & two boys, the entire family of Reth
hunkers down there
and hangs on to each day
as a stutterer might to a frothing, seductively multisyllabic
concoction. No, no, they aren't history,
neither the first fragrant days of the planet
nor the last of collapsing stone. The story is simple,
the furnace goes dead,
kaput, & with no heat
I've been firing up the kitchen stove, folding open its door,
letting it cloud the apartment's atmosphere,
warm & stultifying, sleep-inducing.
When I wake, at twilight, I hear Joe in his van
playing Hendrix. The tapes
his first resort after arguing with Janet.
You would be surprised how much we can hurt.
Even with the windows rolled up
a thumping & wailing seeps out, through the van's back doors,
where Joe has airbrushed his muse, a woman
or cross between a leather queen & Wagnerian Medusa.
This, some genuine Baudelaire
might say, is history, this woman, with her beckoning
enormous breasts from the comic books of my childhood,
her hair braided with flaming snakes, & death-row jewelry.
Even the drops of rain stammer.
You would be surprised how many childhoods each of us has.
The voices we hear can confuse us.
So it seems she speaks like the dead guitarist,
with muffed syntax, a partisan of the left hand.
Demanding I give up
the life inside my head, she says

I have one last chance. Nothing personal,
she tells me, one day
the wind will spill your thoughts, scattering their dust.

The wind won't celebrate your great jihads.

But I love how the wind cries Mary,
so for me there may always be a small room, a mind,
and an argument within, about despair, & the prospects
for getting out. You would be surprised,
there is often mercy. In books,
in the exuberant talk of friends, the building
of garden sculpture out of busted-up motorcycles.
My slow learning means well, but it's slow.
I need to remember the smoke tree,
the five miles the husk rolls through desert
before its seed is worn enough to sprout. Hey Joe?
But Joe Reth has his feet propped on the dash,
and stares into the rain. Right now — the voice
quieter, more balladish & bluesy than fiery
with lighter fluid — I'm being told I could own
the rights to surrender. To be surprised
I could be driving southward. You've driven such a trip,
past the slopes of the Carolinas, or some place
we only partly live, where the unlived life breathes.
You even made a pact with the moths
your windshield & grill avoided, letting yourself see yourself
as they do, benign & generous, neither natural enemy
nor mortal enemy, giftedly naive.
I believe you can help me. I know you,
and some silence has been broken.

FADO

At some point in our lives, let's say someplace
both alarming & companionable, maybe a ledge
almost too high for any return,
we might have to hope
safety descends from the sky
like a long wicker basket dangling
off a grappling hook.
Why not this one? Ours
will be a touch
made out of four — maybe five —
very eager pronouns.
So put down your wine. Why not call it a test,
as if to prove the fact you & I
will never become one creature
can't matter, & every expectation
is not a dress rehearsal for death?
I don't need anything
now. I want
everything, each button loosened
into each breath dreamed. Right now it's likely
I am nearly the equal of a mole,
an eccentric one
who wishes to root down a mountain.
He longs for innocence, as we all do.
My heart feels like an overused paw,
heedless, compulsive, strong
but sore, prone to aching
from days of digging.
It is the mole in me, nearly blind,
a little furtive, shrugging, who lights
the candles, my eyes
sliding from the floor to your face
like one of the singers
of *fado*, those trembling Portuguese tunnelers, those doubters

who puzzle their own doubts, embracers
of the impossible. Now,
put me in danger, your mouth
on mine. And let me
do the same,
for you.

AND CONTINUING

In his eyes & hands, brash assurance.
Delight, masked as a boast,
though he knows his life
adjudged
by force & denials. Max Beckmann,
the Beckmann he himself painted in his mid-30s.
And if the mirror no longer leans in a Bremerhaven attic
wedged between dollhouse & chiffonier,
if it's smashed & exists now only as dust motes
invading a circle of lamp light or altering
a North Sea sunset? Well,
he could never be broken, or dispersed.
In black evening tux, his face thickening,
confronted, a smile aware of its own vanities.
Hair the color of gravity trapped between hammer & anvil.
In his right hand,
half-smoked, a cigar. The curl of smoke
invisible. Insouciant,
amused, & protected by the complete
lack of insouciance that is self-knowledge.
The left hand held away from the jacket,
shooing something off,
palm out, so his wrist shows—
the skin there soft, & embarrassed, by its rosiness,
pulsing lightly, like this woman's neck
as she stands with me waiting
for the traffic signal. Its curve to her collarbone
the place on a body where I love to think
the world begins, there between two or three freckles.
All the world. Starting from this corner,
an Isuzu jeep idling, garter belt
tied to its rearview, & by the cable TV truck
two kids in maroon soccer togs, the crossing guard
loafing, starting with them. Spreading

to include the violence of a summer evening, the MDC pools,
the rib joints, & talk of software licensing
near the horse rider, the bronze
mediocrity of the horse's withers, & past the paddleboats,
the kick boxers,
out beyond them, to fields,
snapdragons, goldenrod, interstates, foxglove,
spreading out like foxglove. And starting here
I promise my pleasure to be so large
as to be right
even if eventually doomed.

LATER HISTORY

No, it isn't so bad being
the tail end of a life-form, & even when it is
over for good, when the planet's rivers
slow to a stop & we are eradicated
along with our hierarchy of golden wasp, conqueror, & clerk,
it still won't be over. Our extermination
will allow us to survive ourselves,
but changed in our ways, humble, less sullen, quickened
like dust driven along by a risen wind.
Each of us a skater
who sidles down a corridor of wind & snowflakes
without loneliness or fear.
I think we will communicate with one another
the way in a bright kitchen on Sundays
a worn & disheveled pajama bottom
sends a message simply by clinging
to a thigh, quietly
but with a sly impunity.
Doubt will defeat itself,
perfectly aware of its own weakness.
All the treaties will be honored, the accords of history,
all the fragrances recalled — of axle grease,
of tangerines — the slapping of sails on the Nile
will be recalled & sung,
while our faces in the mirrors of innumerable bathrooms
no longer will loom up to obsess us.
But sorrow will be unchanged.
So that we may recognize each other.

for Michael McGuire

NOTES

Camus: The passage quoted can be found in the preface to *Lyrical and Critical Essays* by Albert Camus (Vintage/Random House, 1970).

Any Where Out of the World: This poem takes its title from a prose piece by Baudelaire that was published with an English title deliberately misspelled.

Baby Vallejo: The painter Myron Stout was an influential member of the generation of Abstract Expressionists. He became blind later in his life and lived in Provincetown, where we met. Eric Dolphy was a multi-reed virtuoso of the post-bop style — clarinet, flute, and alto sax. He died in 1964.

Earth to Tell of the Beasts: A phrasing in line 13 is borrowed from Adam Zagajewski's "Fate," in *Tremor* (Farrar, Strauss & Giroux, 1985).

Fado: The title refers to a style of Portuguese singing that could be described as resembling American blues, if the blues were written under the influence of Middle Eastern scales.

ABOUT THE AUTHOR

David Rivard's previous book, *Torque*, won the Agnes Lynch Starrett Poetry Prize. Among his many awards are fellowships from the National Endowment for the Arts, the Fine Arts Work Center in Provincetown, and the Massachusetts Cultural Council; a Pushcart Prize, and the Celia B. Wagner Award from the Poetry Society of America. He teaches at Tufts University and in the M.F.A. in Writing Program at Vermont College.

This book was designed by Will Powers.
It is set in Janson type by Stanton Publication Services, Inc.
and manufactured by Quebecor-Fairfield
on acid-free paper. Cover design by Michaela Sullivan.